THE AUTHENTIC LEADER AS SERVANT (ALS)

ALS I COURSE 6
INFLUENCE LEADERSHIP
Attributes, Principles, and Practices

SYLVANUS N. WOSU, Ph.D

THE AUTHENTIC LEADER AS SERVANT
ALS I COURSE 6
Influence Leadership Attributes, Principles, and Practices

© Copyright 2024 by Sylvanus N. Wosu Ph.D.

Printed in the United States of America
ISBN: 979-8-9868665-7-4

All rights reserved. No part of this book may be reproduced or transmitted in any form or by any means, electronic or mechanical, including photocopying, recording, or by any information storage and retrieval system, without permission in writing from the copyright owner.

Bible quotations are from the New King James (NKJV) version of the Bible unless otherwise indicated.

Other versions used in this book are the New International Version (NIV), New Living Translation (NLT), King James Version (KJV), English Standard Version (ESV), and Good News Translation (GNT). Unless otherwise specified, NKJV should be assumed.

The views expressed in this work are solely those of the author and do not necessarily reflect the views of the publisher, and the publisher disclaims any responsibility for them.

To order additional copies of this book, contact:
Proisle Publishing Services LLC
39-67 58th Street, 1st floor
Woodside, NY 11377, USA
Phone: (+1 646-480-0129)
info@proislepublishing.com

PROISLE PUBLISHING

TABLE OF CONTENTS

FOREWORD	XI
ACKNOWLEDGMENTS	XV
DEDICATION	XVII
PREFACE	19

    About Leader As Servant Leadership (LSL) Model -------------------------- 22
    About the Authentic Leader as Servant (ALS) --------------------------------- 25
    About the ALS Courses -- 26

CHAPTER 1
UNDERSTANDING LEADERSHIP ATTRIBUTES   35

    Functional Definitions --- 35
    Comparisons With Other Works -- 40
    Principle of Leadership Attribute --- 42
    Authentic Leadership Attributes --- 43
    Summary 1 Understanding Leadership Process ------------------------------- 49

CHAPTER 2
INFLUENCE LEADERSHIP ATTRIBUTE   53

    Characteristics of Influence Attribute ------------------------------------- 54
    Principle of Leadership Influence Attribute ----------------------------- 57
    Summary 2 Influence Leadership Attribute ------------------------------- 58

CHAPTER 3
DEVELOPING THE INFLUENCE-MODEL   61

    Modeling Influence with Your Assets --------------------------------------- 62
    Influence from Passion and Convictions ---------------------------------- 62
    Influence from Your Spiritual Presence ----------------------------------- 63
    Summary 3 Developing the Influence-Model ----------------------------- 63

CHAPTER 4
DEVELOPING THE INFLUENCE-AUTHORITY   67

    Influence by Autority with conviction--------------------------------------- 67
    Encouraging and Inspiring Confidence ------------------------------------- 67
    Discrete use of authority to influence ------------------------------------- 68
    Purposeful use of facts to influence change ---------------------------- 69
    Summary 4 Developing the Influence-Authority ------------------------ 70

CHAPTER 5
DEVELOPING INFLUENCE-CONNECTION   73

Building Connections to influence ------- 73
Connecting to Hopes and Aspirations ------- 74
Making Friends to Connect ------- 75
Valuing People as Assets ------- 76
Summary 5 Developing Influence- Connection ------- 77

TOPIC INDEX   81
REFERENCES   83

FOREWORD

The modern world today is obsessed with standardization and modalities. As a result, in the realm of leadership, many books have spout associated leadership theories and models and explain them as the path to follow. However, the critical dimensions that distinguish the effectiveness of any leadership process are the values and attribute the leader brings to the table; desired change is influenced by leadership styles or standards. These many standards and theories of leadership often are not in step with the changing times or the followers' needs. The trend is a bit like stocking different kinds of foods in a grocery store and expecting that they will meet everybody's needs the same way and at all times. Aisles are packed with varieties of food with expiration dates in the future, but getting the best deal on the products is what really matters to those who buy and use the products

In many ways, this is the state of leadership in the modern world. Increasingly, even leaders of public institutions are tasked with turning a profit for themselves or the organization they serve. The idea of a "leader" seems to float uneasily alongside the ranks of fundraisers or profit raisers in contrast to any kind of role model for followers or employees. That which is knowable, measurable, and marketable has surpassed the difficult intangibility of strong moral leadership attributes as the central guideline for achievement and success.

In this complicated space, Dr. Sylvanus Wosu introduces his complex idea of the Leader as a Servant Leadership, which is in this book, modeled on Christian tradition. Like all intricate ideas, Dr. Wosu's central point depends on a paradox: a person is best qualified to lead when he or she is most ready to serve. This paradox has been monopolized rhetorically by "public servants" who often serve either self-interest or the interests of specific lobbies. The Authentic Leader as Servant penetrates past the superficial concept of "serving" and details the internal state of true servitude or Servanthood.

While the book is primarily focused on the Christian model of leadership attributes such as discipleship, empathy, affection, and Servanthood, it does so not merely on the grounds of blind faith, but rather via numerous contemporary sociological and business-driven studies on how leaders should seek a leader-follower relationship that is simultaneously productive and nurturing. Dr. Wosu's most piercing insights always involve this secular–Christian dialogue. This book demonstrates that Christ's model for leadership is one that may exist successfully outside the confines of a faith relationship; it places the values of Christ's religious significance in leadership at the center of the framework. It is clear from Dr. Wosu's generous own life story of faith—a faith tested by humbling difficulties—is at the center of both his orientation and motivation for writing.

In language that is so concise, it is often illustrated in mathematical formulas; Dr. Wosu explains the deep structural integrity of Christ's Leader as the Servant Leadership model. One could imagine leaders of any doctrine benefiting from the analyses contained in these pages. The book's message repeatedly encourages the reader to imagine a scenario or reflect on memories and personal experiences to prove or test its many points. Thus, the book depends on a form of praxis, a lesson that could be or has been enacted, by the participating reader. I am very impressed at the volume and level of thinking of the author. Parts of the book involve his personal story, which is especially riveting. I cannot imagine what he had to endure, which he referred to as a" wilderness walk," to accomplish the goal he set for himself. His life stories on these pages are inspiring and stimulating.

In this way, the text eschews dogmatism in favor of the self-discovery Socratic Method of teaching and learning. The reader is not badgered into complying with a religious objective but is rather asked to consider the applicability of difficult biblical concepts in relation to modern life. It is a fascinating and very thought-provoking read.

Hence, the book does not seek to make the leader a servant, a cookie-cutter corporate buzzword, but rather asks the reader to imagine him or herself interacting with a range of concepts. One of Dr. Wosu's great strengths is his reservation when it comes to forcing his reading's interpretation on the material he presents.

The book parallels Biblical and modern leadership scenarios in ways that consistently provoke thought, and while it is clear Dr. Wosu has his particular leadership style; the space for the reader's own thoughts is always left open.

The book could not have been written in any other way with integrity. Its format and formulas are offered to the reader of the leader as a servant role that it analyzes in its pages. To find a text that instructs from this humble position is profoundly refreshing in a genre that is often packaged inside a cover with a sizeable picture of the "modest" author, smiling egotistically beneath a name spelled out in large, gold lettering. Throughout its pages, this text feels as if it serves the reader.

In the end, this is the most satisfying aspect of the book. There is no standardized approach to achieving successful leadership. There is no promise of power and a bigger payday; in fact, the book often proffers just the opposite. The reader is not encouraged to devalue the experience of leadership by finding some economic metric for marking success but is rather asked to think deeply about the most basic elements of internal and social interaction within the framework of a Christian tradition. What this means will be different for every reader. Indeed, even in the context of single chapters, I found myself questioning or re-evaluating moments of my own life. This book serves; it doesn't feel like filling in multiple-choice questions, staring at a wall of flavorless grocery products, or hearing the endless servant promises of today's political scene. It feels like a humble invitation to consider a single paradoxical element of a profoundly productive tradition.

-Tobias Bates

Acknowledgments

A book on leadership attributes as aspects of Servant Leadership sprouted from the wealth of knowledge and the inspirations of many other leaders. Their writings were sources of inspiration, challenges, and examples of excellence to emulate.

Dr. Enefaa N. Wosu, my wife and life partner, for her love, commitment, and prayer support, especially during those long night hours I was not there for her and her constant reminder of who I must be as a leader-servant. Without her support, forbearance, wisdom, and encouragement, this project would not have been completed; I say, thank you very much.

And to God alone be all the glory and honor for the divine inspiration and guidance in initiating and completing this life-transforming book project.

Dedication

I humbly submit this book back unto the gracious hands of God who inspired the writings through His Holy Spirit!

I dedicate this book to my virtuous wife of 45 years, Rev. (Dr.) Enefaa Wosu whose spiritual leadership is an important gateway to our home, and to our four wonderful children—Prof. Eliada Wosu-Griffin EL, HeCareth, Tamuno-Emi, and Chidinma. From them all, I learnt what it meant to be a leader-servant. I could not be blessed with better teachers.

PREFACE

What characteristics did Biblical leaders like the Apostle Paul, Moses, Joshua, and Nehemiah as servants of their people display outwardly that distinguished them from other leaders, both then and now? The Apostle Paul kept his focus to *emulate* Christ and endured all the infirmities and persecutions he suffered to complete his goal to preach the gospel of Jesus Christ. He inspired Timothy and others through his effective *discipleship* leadership to imitate him as he emulated Christ. Moses' outward display of his *trust* in God's power earned him a good level of trust from the people and empowered him for the mission of delivery of God's children from bondage in Egypt; he had to *reproduce* himself in Joshua to complete the mission. But the greatest of them was Jesus Christ, who humbly sacrificed His life to finish the work of redemption. In His *Servanthood*, commitment, and love for the people, He became the ultimate *model* of a leader as a servant to *emulate*.

Let's consider for a moment secular leaders in these current times! For example, think of Henry Ford, who founded the successful Ford Motor Company; Bill Gates who created the global empire that is Microsoft; Albert Einstein, who in many ways is synonymous with a genius for his contributions to modern physics; Abraham Lincoln, remembered as one of the greatest presidents and leaders of United States; and many others like these we cannot mention. What did all these leaders have in common? What propelled them to turn their initial failures or challenges into eventual successes? None had a direct mentor or inherited any fortune from their parents. Nevertheless, they all eventually succeeded. These people can be distinguished from others based on their self-will to succeed, their self-confidence and belief in themselves, their self-determination, and their perseverance, among other characteristics. The distinguishing characteristics displayed externally in service or relationships toward others are the outward functional attributes that define that leader.

Think about yourself as a student, faculty member, or that new executive. What was it that made your journey to success different and even great? Students and colleagues, when they see or hear about my display of what I have referred to as the 'wilderness walk of faith', have asked me to share the critical attitudinal elements that made me remain inwardly resilient and undaunted and yet outwardly joyful in the difficulties I had faced. This book is the result of those reflections. Let me explain one such teaching moment.

Many years ago, sitting in my research lab on a Saturday morning trying to finish writing my dissertation, a fellow graduate student walked into the room to talk with me. He was contemplating terminating his graduate studies. He was a privileged single male student but felt the load was just too much.

"Sylvanus," he asked, with seriousness in his eyes, "your research advisor suggested that I should ask you, 'what is it that makes you tick?'.'What is it about you that makes you joyful and at peace with yourself and determined to finish, no matter the situations and high expectations we face in this department?"

What he asked me were deeply reflective questions, but I was willing and excited to answer them. Even so, before I do, let's look at the context. At that period in my life, I had four little children as a graduate student; in fact, more children than any of the faculties at that time, except for one faculty member who had eight children. I received little or no support from the department. I was then an international alien, did not qualify for financial aid, and was not given any research assistant position. I was, therefore, self-supported with two off-campus part-time jobs. I joked at being a minority of minorities, the only student in the department with such a label,—but I was self-willed to succeed. My adaptability attribute, coupled with perseverance and resilience, was all that I needed to succeed despite the odds against me. In every exam, homework assignment, or project I had to compete with students with full financial aid, plus they had nothing to distract their attention from their studies. I lived with the attitude that using disadvantages as an excuse was not an option. Aspiring to earn my Ph.D. was a life dream, and I was willing to give my ultimate best to actualize that dream even in the face of challenges. The choice was mine!

So I looked at my classmate and all I could see was a student striding through a valley through which I also walked. He needed me to show him how to walk the walk, to empathize with him. To answer his question, I smiled, not that I wanted to, but because it was just who I was. The joy he attributed to me was an overflow of my appreciation of God's grace that His life in me was externally manifesting His light to bless someone else. It was a great teaching moment; I capitalized on it to tell my classmate that my joy was not about me. He could see physically but about He who was in me, he could not see in the flesh; I needed him to know that I was just showing forth His life in me. At first, my classmate did not understand the spiritual prose or metaphor I was using. He looked surprised but open to hearing more.

I did not ask if he was a Christian. However, right on my desk was my small green pocket Bible. I opened to 2 Corinthians 12:9 (NIV) and handed it to him to read. As he read the passage: "But he said to me, 'My grace is sufficient for you, for my power is made perfect in weakness.' Therefore, I will boast all the more gladly about my weaknesses, so that Christ's power may rest on me," I noticed how absorbed he was in the words

He looked astonished and read it again, this time silently. "This is interesting, but what does this mean?" He asked. I took his question to mean, "How does this relate to my question?"

I explained to my friend that the external attitudes he or my advisors saw in me that warranted the question, "What makes you tick" were inspired by my inner value system based on my faith in this same Christ and His teachings. My desire to manifest His life and self-confidence is all because of what He has promised in His word if I believed. I have believed His words and have gained self-determination and faith to make the right choices through Him for my life, and his spirit has given me perseverance and resilience to focus on finishing strong in pursuit of any goal. "With that faith, I have continued, more passionately and excitedly; I can look at my challenges and vulnerabilities and delight joyfully in them, even as an alien minority of minorities! His grace and power have empowered me to do all things I want to do. That is what makes me tick," I explained.

He looked at me as if he got his answer. "Wow, thanks!" he said, looking inspired and ready to face his challenges. As we concluded with a prayer, and he stood up to leave, I pointed empathetically to his face and said, "If I made it despite my challenges, you have absolutely no excuse but to persevere to complete your studies; you can make it too!"

It is fitting to report that this encounter with my classmate transformed his will and determination to continue. Yes, he was encouraged and went on to complete his graduate studies. He emulated self-will and perseverance from the example of the most vulnerable of all students in the department.

The inner value system of a Leader-Servant is founded not only on his faith but his self-will, coupled with self-leadership; it is the greatest mentor who can turn any situation into an inconceivable success. Self-will is the primary driver for determination, resilience, and perseverance. It is what wakes you up in the morning to ask for strength to do whatever it is you are setting out to do. Based on my life walk of faith, I can state with absolute certainty that faith is the unseen assuredness that can empower you to turn your life's probable impossibilities into great and improbable possibilities.

ABOUT LEADER AS SERVANT LEADERSHIP (LSL) MODEL

Looking at the testimony above, do you know the source that energizes the characteristics you display outside and how your inner self is related to what others see outside? What distinguishes you from others is what combines to define your attributes! As a follower, can you identify the characteristics that distinguish your leaders? As an executive, how do you base your evaluation of yourself? Or how do you evaluate that brand-new manager or new youth director you want to hire? To what do you compare the individual's qualities when you look at his CV? What is the basis of your measure? Do you know if you are a substantial leader? These personal questions and much more are the subjects of this two-volume book, 'The Authentic Leader as Servant Part I: The Outward Leadership Attributes, Principles, and Practices', is written in two parts; the second part 'The Leader as Servant Leadership Model. Part II'; deals with the Inner Strength Leadership Attributes, Principles, and Practices.

When we think about today's corporate greed, deepening divide between the haves and have-not, gridlock in political systems, conflicts and wars, high divorce rates, and the rich young ruler in the Bible, it is easy to agree that all these people share a few things in common: self-centeredness, pride, lack of compassion, and greed. There is a great need in today's suffering world for leader-servants who display leadership attributes. These attributes should be oriented toward selfless service to others. Indeed, our world is increasingly drifting away from global serving reality toward the self and apathy. The most credible message or model for a possible solution to this dilemma and the answer to several complex leadership questions can be found in the foundation of the ultimate leader-servant, Jesus Christ. This book defines the Leader as Servant Leadership attribute as the combined acts of two or more distinctive functional leadership characteristics exhibited in service and relationship toward others. There is no better time than now for a book that presents comprehensive and irrevocable facts and principles regarding how to develop effective attributes of the leader-servant.

The Leader as Servant Leadership Model
My first book on this subject, The Leader as Servant Leadership Model, explains that Jesus' servant leadership model is based on the notion of a Leader as a Servant and not on a Servant as Leader. There are four distinct differences between a Servant as Leader (Servant-leader) and the Leader as Servant (leader--servant) models. It is pertinent to highlight them here to connect to this book, Authentic Leader as Servant.

A Leader as Servant is a leader first. The leader–servant as a leader does not in the line of duty go projecting or lording his or her power and authority over others but is the person to lead the process of influencing desired changes in others through his humble example of being a servant or having a serviceable attitude toward others. He or she is a serving leader, not a lording leader. He leads as a servant by putting others' needs above his own needs and rights. Jesus emphasized the word "as" meaning that the leader (the Master) chooses to serve as a servant even though he is the leader. A leader–servant emulates Jesus, who gave up all rights, and emptied and expended Himself on His followers. He empowered them to become more like Him. A leader-servant is known as a leader first but is seen as a great leader by his humble attendant heart and acts of service to others. His greatness comes from his ability to put others above himself.

Leader as Servant is a Biblical Concept. The model or image of a humble serving leader motivated Jesus' disciples to see that if their master could do this for them, they must also be able to do it for others. Jesus clearly demonstrated the process of leader-as-servant leadership. In some cases, He chose to serve by leading when He wanted to create the image or model of the leader-servant in certain acts. In other cases, He chose to lead by serving, when he showed care and empathy toward the people and led the disciples to see empathy as a leadership attribute.

Leader as Servant is an Authentic Leadership Model to follow. The Leader as the Servant leadership model intentionally positions Jesus as an original model of a leader to follow.

He was serving His disciples to demonstrate that the process of becoming a great leader was earned through humble acts of service to others; He made them understand that He was empowering them to succeed Him as leader-servants through service to others. The result was an incomparable legacy of leadership that changed their communities. The fact that Jesus relinquished his rights or shared His power did not diminish His power and influence. In fact, his influence increased at least 11 X 100%, if we ignore the one case of Judas.

The Leader as Servant Transforms Organizational Culture. The proposed LSL model seeks to transform and sustain the community or organization by instilling key leadership values or "leadership presence" among followers or an organization's members. Change is sustained when everyone in the organization takes ownership of the change. Rather than focusing on leading more followers to be great followers who conform to the organizational culture, LSL seeks to lead and empower better leaders to be distinguished leaders and community builders.

There are four distinctions, which clearly differentiate many of the existing servants as Leader-based philosophies in relation to servant leadership from my LSL model. Even in the corporate or institutional worlds, there is nothing better than Jesus on which to base Servant Leadership. There is nothing more authentic and impacting than the servant leadership modeled by the life and teachings of Jesus Christ.

The LSL model uses exploratory questions, scenarios, and graphic visualizations to excite critical thinking in ways no other book on this subject has yet attempted. Several personal testimonies of my wilderness walk of faith with God are used to connect the reader to real-life experiences of the concepts discussed. The riveting effect is that the text engages and encourages the reader to walk through the experiences presented. The aim is to inspire the reader spiritually, mentally, and professionally with this far-reaching exposition on the subject of servant leadership.

ABOUT THE AUTHENTIC LEADER AS SERVANT (ALS)

The *Authentic Leader as Servant* argues that no leadership model is as authentic, other-centered, able to build communities, and productive and service-oriented as the model of our ultimate leader-servant, Jesus Christ. No source can provide a better point of reference than that provided in the Bible. Hence, this book aims to be more than just a text on leadership; it hopes to be a personal discovery for those who aspire to develop effective leadership attributes that grow leaders as servants who ultimately develop thriving other-centered communities. This book presents a comprehensive, biblically-based study regarding how to develop these attributes and how they are applied in a servant leadership process. In this biblical context and for clarity, Servant Leadership means *Leader-as-Servant Leadership*. A *leader-servant* refers to a *leader as a servant*, which is distinct from a servant-leader or servant as leader.

Leader as Servant Leadership attributes are shaped by the Leadership's Inner Value system, which consists of character, motivation, and commitment. The *Authentic Leader as Servant* is presented as a necessary resource to complement my *The Leader as Servant Leadership (LSL) Model*. The LSL model integrates a transformative leadership framework and interactive dimensions of Servant Leadership. Leader as Servant Leadership is a process in which a leader, in his leadership position, purposefully chooses to put others' rights and needs above his positional rights and personal needs. He then serves, enables, and empowers followers for growth that builds a thriving organization. The LSL model looks at the predominant Servant Leadership concepts and shares how they compare with biblical principles on how we should lead and be led.

ABOUT THE ALS COURSES

The three books, *LSL Model* and *The Authentic Leader as Servant (*Parts I and II), together demonstrate that with today's global visions to reach people of all races and cultures, now is the time for an authentic servant's heart of service. Those visions and the leadership processes are most effective with the appropriate leadership attributes centered more on people than on the organization, principles regarding how to develop effective attributes of leader-servant.

The ALS I and II combined presented twenty leaders as servant leadership attributes. The series of ALS courses supply training guide to understand, develop, and practice the attributes in a leadership process. Each course is independent and self-contained and does not depend on completing any other course in the series of 20 courses. It is, however strongly recommended, in fact a must read, that chapters 1 and 2 in each series be covered as they lay the foundation of LSL model on which ALS is based.

ALS (Parts I & II) Course Layout

The *Authentic Leader as Servant (ALS)* leadership (parts I and II) book has been broken down into 20 courses in workbook format to achieve three goals 1) Self-discovery of the acts of developing the attribute under review in the course, 2) deeper understanding of the principles, research and biblical teaching behind the attributes, and 3) Learning the strategies for practicing the attributes.

Instruction

The set of questions following each chapter are designed to serve as a guide to discover, explore, and practice the essential ALS leadership attributes, principles, and practices in leadership process. The questions are comprehensive review based on the content of this specific chapter only.

To maximize the learning outcomes, the learner must read through this chapter and sections. Some referenced scriptures in the book are repeated in the summaries for added review if needed, even though they were discussed in the section in which they apply.

> The exercises that follow each chapter will help you in not only understanding your own strength and weaknesses in your acts of the attribute but will guide you in developing practical strategies you can apply in self-leadership process or helping others grow in leadership
>
> All answers to the questions are contained in the associated chapter or sections; consultation of new sources, except for the reference scriptures, is not needed. Thus, it is expected that you answer the questions after you have read the associated section or chapter of the workbook. The scripture or other references cited are only for references as they already discussed in the book

---

ALS I Course 1: Affection Leadership Attribute—*Affection flows from a person to produce positive emotions for the well-being of another person.*

An average person will define the word "love" in the sense that affection is a characteristic of love. Nevertheless, that definition clouds the functional meaning of affection as an attribute of a leader-servant. Affection is a love action intentionally given to someone to create favorable emotion. We experience a positive emotion when we receive or give affection. In his acts of affection, the Apostle Paul communicated to the Corinthian Christians how he spoke to them freely with an open heart, because it was an important way to give affection (2 Corinthians 6:11-13). He also spoke of longing for them with the affection of Jesus Christ (Philippians 1:8); an affection that needs to be mutual (1 Peter 1:7). How is the affection leadership attribute an outward leadership attribute? This course explores this and other questions to discover the characteristics of affection attributes and to formulate a functional principle based on the expected outcome of affection and the effective use of these attributes in leadership.

ALS I Course 2: Discipleship Leadership Attribute- *Discipleship transforms and empowers followers for service leadership that grows communities.*

Discipleship as an act of developing a follower toward a specific goal is an important function of leadership to equip others to lead. *Discipleship transforms and empowers followers for service leadership that grows communities*. A disciple is a follower who willingly chooses to follow the master and submits to his discipleship and authority. In that regard, Jesus wanted all his followers to be his disciples and ambassadors because a disciple is always a follower. Organizationally, a follower could be a junior employee, any employee in a brand-new department, a new younger faculty, or just any person that needs to be guided through a journey of professional growth and good success. This course focuses on the general growth of followers through the acts of discipleship and presents the critical characteristics of discipleship as a leadership outward attribute. Functional definitions of leadership discipleship attributes and its principle will be presented based on those characteristics. Each characteristic will be discussed in detail with emphasis on strategies of how they can be further developed or practiced as a part of the servant leadership process.

ALS I Course 3: Emulation Leadership Attribute—*A great leader-servant outwardly and positively inspires a pattern of good works for others to follow.*

To emulate is to strive to be like someone else or to follow someone else's example by imitating something that inspires you about that person. This course evaluates how to learn from someone good leadership qualities to develop yours. How did you use what you learned from following the footstep of your hero to grow your leadership qualities. Jesus in the scripture modeled humility and Servanthood he wanted his disciples to develop same qualities. Emulation as a leadership attribute shares some characteristics with transformative leadership, where a leader intentionally conveys a clear vision of a goal, inspires the passion for the work toward the goal, and motivates the followers to follow. As a leader, how do you model a characteristic behavior for someone to follow or develop? How is Leadership Emulation Leadership Attribute an outward leadership attribute? This course explores this and other questions to discover the characteristics of affection attributes and to formulate a functional principle based on the expected outcome of effective use of these attributes in leadership.

ALS I Course 4: Generosity Leadership Attribute: *Generosity is an outward measure of the level of sacrifice, what is shared, or the impact a giving makes, not just the size of the giving*

Generosity can be defined as "the *habit of giving* without expecting anything in return. It can involve offering time, assets, or talents to aid someone in need." Such habits can include spending your personal money, time, and/or labor for the welfare of others or expending (suffering or being consumed or spending) for others' well-being. When political leaders or Board members 'vote their conscience' on important issues that affect others, what is that "conscience" and how do such leaders contribute to the welfare of others? How can you, "Do all you can, with what you have, in the time you have, in the place where you are" for the betterment of humanity All giving to help humanity is crucial to help meet the needs of the most vulnerable of God's children, as demonstrated by God as attribute of God, In this course, we will explore what distinguishes a leader's act of giving from his inside intentions. The key leadership characteristics of generosity will be discussed with respect to Servant-Leadership generosity Attributes and Principles and the details how a leader-servant can develop those characteristics and then effectively practice service leadership.

ALS I Course 5: Healing-Care Leadership Attribute: *Comforting others in any trouble with the comfort with which God comforts us, brings healing-wholeness*

What is healing Care and what does it mean in practical terms to you as a leader? Effective leadership begins with an emotionally and spiritually healthy leader who can reconcile and bring comfort to the followers, irrespective of followers' feelings (good or bad) toward the leader. The healing attribute and personal security complement each other. You must have the capacity for self-healing and individual security if you are to meet others' comforts. Personal security provides the infrastructure to support leaders in adversity and heal others that are hurting. A leader's or a group's success is measured by the strength of the weakest member or follower in the group or team… Healing is one of the most abstract and least understood attributes in leadership, and yet one of the most important. The key distinguishing characteristics will be explored to formulate a working definition and principle of leadership healing-care attributes based on those characteristics. Each characteristic will be discussed in detail with emphasis on strategies of how they can be further developed or practiced by a leader-servant as part of the servant leadership process.

ALS I Course 6: Influence Leadership Attribute-*The true measure of leadership success in affecting desired change in conduct, performance, and relational connections in others is influence*

Leadership is an integrative process in which a person applies appropriate (leadership) attributes to guide and influence the desired attitudinal changes in others toward accomplishing a particular goal. Eight five percent of CEOs of top companies surveyed on their climb to leadership ladder said they were "influenced by another leader," compared to 10% and 5% for "natural gifting" and "result of a crisis," respectively. When we consider influence as a servant leadership attribute, we are talking about a distinguishing leadership characteristic that displays on the outside what a leader is inside, influence takes on a deeper meaning. In this course, the key leadership characteristics of influence will be identified and explored from research to frame definitions of the Servant-Leadership influence attribute and principle. Based on those characteristics, the key outcomes of effective leadership influence l how a leader-servant can develop those characteristics and then effectively practice service leadership.

ALS I Course 7: Persuasion Leadership Attribute—*The means of transforming others to a new perspective is through empathetic persuasion.*

Persuasion attribute affords the leader the capacity to convince his followers or others to believe and engage in a new idea or goal through encouragement rather than using his positional authority or intimidation. Because members of the group may already have their views on an issue, the leader must carefully approach persuasion as a learning process to avoid conflicts or polarizing the group. He must unify the diversity of views to get buy-in and willingness to agree and follow. The leader-servant primarily relies on making decisions within an organization based on persuasion rather than positional authority. In other words, you will never hear the Leader-servant say, "Do it because I am the boss, and I say to." This particular element offers one of the clearest distinctions between the traditional authoritarian model of leadership and the concept of Servant leadership. In this course, we will explore the technique of convincing rather than coercing as one of the most effective ways a leader-servant can build consensus within groups. Key characteristics of persuasion leadership attribute will be found, fully discussed, and modeled from the examples in the lives of other leaders.

ALS I Course 8: Reproduction Leadership Attribute—*Great leaders produce successors for legacy and greater courses as an expected product of an effective leadership reproduction.*

In his book, *360 Degree Leader,* John C. Maxwell says, "Great leaders don't use people so they can win. They lead people so they can all lead together." Such great leaders, like Jesus, Moses, Paul, and others developed other leaders through a process of reproduction. Is it possible for leaders of today to reproduce their vision in others so that can lead and build a legacy together? The answer to this question is of course yes. However, the effectiveness of a leader duplicating his leadership qualities in a follower depends on the leadership reproduction attribute of the leader. This course explores the distinguishing characteristics of reproduction as an outward attribute in servant leadership. Functional definitions of leadership reproduction attribute and its principle will be presented based on those characteristics. Each characteristic of reproduction attributes will be discussed in detail with emphasis on strategies of how they can be further developed or practiced by a leader-servant as part of the servant leadership process.

ALS I Course 9: Servanthood Leadership Attribute— *A leader-servant is most qualified to lead when ready to serve as a servant for the growth of others.*

The last time you engaged in a practical act of service on the job, at home, church, or in your community, what were the key elements in that act of service? Did you serve because you wanted to and chose to serve? Or was it because someone asked you to? The ultimate goal is for the leader's life to positively transform many lives in his or her community of followers. Consider the New Testament teachings of Jesus, who demonstrated the ultimate Leader as Servant Leadership. Jesus equated greatness to serving unpretentiously (humbly, as would a child), and He equated leading with choosing to serve others. That is the first affirmative test of authenticity for this attribute. What were the distinguishing characteristics that enabled you to serve? How is the Leadership Servanthood an outward leadership attribute? This course will give answers and meanings to these and personal reflective questions to discover the distinguishing characteristics of The Leadership Servanthood attribute. Functional definitions of The Leadership Servanthood attribute and principle will be provided based on the identified characteristics. Readers will benefit from numerous techniques, personal examples, empirical case study, and applications of the concepts.

ALS I Course 10: Trust-Integrity Leadership Attribute—*True leadership trust produces assured trustee's confidence and readiness to follow based on the credibility, competence, and shared relational connections of the trusted.*

A study examined more than 75 key components of employee satisfaction in top leadership and found that trust and confidence was the single most reliable predictor of employee satisfaction in an organization. This course will examine the results of the above study with respect to servant leadership, and how a leader-servant increases the satisfaction of the followers in an organization. When the organization is going through some challenges, how can a leader be credible in helping the followers understand the company's mission and strategy? How can he share information on how the company or institution, or department is doing and how the followers or employees will be affected? Suppose the organization's strategy is not aligned with its inner value or character, how does the leader build trust in followers or earn trust from them? Organizational leadership trust has been defined by as "an employee's willingness to take a risk for a leader with the expectation that, in exchange, the leader will behave in some desired way." The course will examine how the element of reliance and confidence in the actions of the trusted and organization are characterized by a combination of Competence (Can they do the job?), Benevolence (Do they care about me?), and Integrity (Are they honest?).

Referenced Scriptures

A variety of Bible translations from over 11,200 original Hebrew, Aramaic, and Greek words to about 6,000 English words do exist with variations in meanings and emphases. I am not a biblical scholar and do not pretend to be one; Hence, I have avoided researching the roots of these words and personally prefer New King James Version (NKJV). I have intentionally used other translations for three main reasons; first, to allow for increased impact and alignment of words to the most desired meaning and emphasis in the concepts being addressed. Second, I wanted new and personal discovery of meanings from translations with which I have not been familiar. And third, I wanted to allow readers who may desire translations other than the NKJV the benefit of their preferred translations. Hence, in addition to the NKJV, other translations used in the book include New International Version (NIV), New Living Translation (NLT), King James Version (KJV), English Standard Version (ESV), and Good News Translation (GNT). Unless otherwise specified, NKJV should be assumed.

Sylvanus Nwakanma Wosu

CHAPTER 1
UNDERSTANDING LEADERSHIP ATTRIBUTES

Leadership attribute is the combined acts of two or more distinctive functional leadership characteristics exhibited in service and relationship toward others.

The starting point of our discussion is the understanding of the key functional definitions and concepts that describe the theme of this book. In general, 1 will define leadership as an integrative process in which a person applies appropriate attributes to guide and influence the sought-after attitudinal changes in others toward accomplishing a particular goal. Specifically, the Leader as Servant Leadership is a process in which a leader intentionally chooses to put the follower's rights and needs above his positional rights and personal needs, and serves, enables, and empowers them for desired spiritual and professional growth that builds thriving communities.

FUNCTIONAL DEFINITIONS

In the context of these definitions, I will begin the descriptions of the leadership attributes of an authentic leader-servant by offering a functional definition of Leadership Attributes, and showing how that definition differs from those of Leadership Character, Characteristics, and Traits.

Leadership Character is the sum total of personal qualities in leadership, such as honesty, values, vision, trust, and so on that make up the moral capital of the leader; Leadership character should describe who the leader is inside or the leader's basic personality traits.

The Leadership Characteristics describe the distinctive characteristics or features of a leader, such as attitudes, competencies, skills, and specific experiences that go beyond his character (personality). Leadership characteristics determine how (through skills and competencies) the leader leads or take actions in the process of leadership in any particular situation;

The Leadership traits are the distinguishing leadership characteristics of a leader (these are things that define his leadership characteristics), which differentiate from personality traits... Leadership traits are the set of characteristics that define a particular leader's leadership. This means that a leadership characteristic is a trait when it is a unique characteristic of the leader.

Leadership Attributes, unlike leadership character, characteristics, and traits, is *a leadership attribute and the combined act of two or more distinctive functional leadership characteristics exhibited in service and relationship toward others* or traits externally displayed in action toward others. All leadership attributes grow out of the leadership inner value system but can be externally displayed predominantly as an outbound or outward attribute or both:

1. **Outbound Attributes:** These are distinctive outward-bound attributes emanating from the inner strength of the leader to support external conduct in service and relationships toward others. They form the internal core functional qualities that motivate or enhance the outward manifestation of the inside character toward others. The outbound attribute such as listening and vision, for example, are the direct results of the inner values of the leader such as patience, hearing, love, humility, or all the fruits of the spirit.

2. **Outward Attributes:** These are distinctive functional outward outer visible attributes emanating from the richness of the outbound and inner values of the leader. For example, external attributes such as Servanthood, emulation/modeling, empathy, etc. are outflows from the leader who will directly impact the follower. Outward attributes can be enriched by the outbound (inner) attributes. As shown in Figure 1, the outward attributes in general form the outer core of

functional attributes in the leader as servant leadership, but they can share some overlapping functions with the outbound attributes.

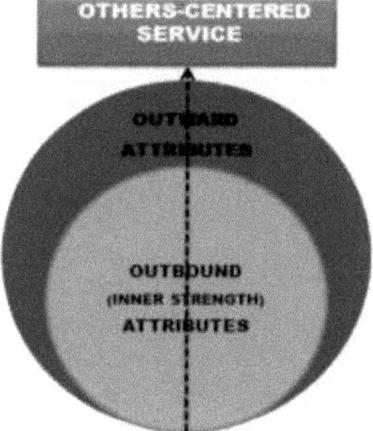

Figure 1.1. Servant leadership functional attributes

In summary, a leadership attribute is more than an ability or a characteristic; it is making those characteristics or abilities functional as part of how the leader acts (his habits) in service to others and applying those characteristics (beyond just having them) in personal and service relations to others. The character or known characteristic defines some aspects of your abilities or who you are inside— e.g. honest, humble, brave, etc. Your attribute, on the other hand, defines your habits; a display of how you use your characteristics, or the actions you exhibit toward others because of who you are inside. For example, empathy as a leadership characteristic becomes a leadership attribute if the followers can distinguish the leader's acts or habits of empathy, such as walking through with his followers in their state of suffering to bring wholeness; otherwise, it is just a characteristic or ability. Leadership attributes toward others are what impact the followers' and the organizational growth more than ability and competence.

In addressing one of the self-righteous hypocritical attributes of servitude leadership, Jesus called leader-servants to be "inside-out" leaders that reflect credibility; indeed, leaders should not appear outwardly righteous when they are full of hypocrisy and lawlessness in their hearts. He was describing "inside–out" as an authentic leadership attribute measured by the display of credibility a leadership attribute!

The measuring stick of a leader-servant is Jesus Christ. We measure ourselves unto the measure of the status of the fullness of Christ (Ephesians 4:13).

The leadership attributes of an authentic leader as a servant are encapsulated in **SERVANT/SERVING LEADERSHIP** are listed in Table 1.1, and defined in Table 1.2: *Servanthood, Emulation, Responsibility, Vision, Navigation, Adaptability, Trust, Listening, Empathy, Affection, Discipleship, Encouragement, Reproduction, Stewardship, Healing-Care, Initiation, Integrity,* and *Persuasion*. Other support attributes include *Influence, Courage, and Generosity*.

The attributes have been separated into Outward and Outbound (Inner Strength) leadership Attributes. As shown in Table 1.1, each of these attributes has three or more leadership characteristics. As such, more than 65 leadership characteristics are covered in these 20 attributes. For example, a leader's Servanthood leadership attribute is characterized by his willing servant's heart of selfless role humility, sacrifice, and submissiveness. The more these are present in a leader, the more effective the servant leadership.

Table 1.1: The functional leader-servant leadership Outbound (Inner Strength) and Outward attributes

	LEADER-SERVANT LEADERSHIP ATTRIBUTES			INNER STRENGTH ATTRIBUTES	OUTWARD ATTRIBUTES
S	Servanthood	**L**	Listening	Adaptability	Affection
E	Emulation	**E**	Empathy	Courage	Discipleship
R	Responsibility	**A**	Affection	Empathy	Emulation
V	Vision	**D**	Discipleship	Encouragement	Generosity
A	Adaptability	**E**	Encouragement	Initiation	Healing–Care
N	Navigation	**R**	Reproduction	Listening	Influence
T	Trust	**S**	Stewardship	Navigation	Persuasion
I	Influence	**H**	Healing–Care	Responsibility	Reproduction
G	Generosity	**I**	Initiation	Stewardship	Servanthood
C	Courage	**P**	Persuasion	Vision	Trust/Integrity

The list does not assume that a leader has to be excellent in all attributes or even have all of them to be an effective Leader–Servant. However, the more of these attributes the leader displays in his acts of service toward others, the more productive he or she will be, and the further his impact on the followers and organization. The table also shows that two or more attributes can share common characteristics, which can be applied or observed in different contexts. For example, a leader's ability to inspire followers can be seen in his acts of discipleship, empowerment, an.d encouragement attributes in the context in which these attributes apply. Each attribute is exhibited either as a part of the outbound inner strength attribute of a leader or a part of the outward attribute. Table 1.1 is not an exhaustive list of attributes; in fact, there are hundreds of such attributes. This is just the starting point.

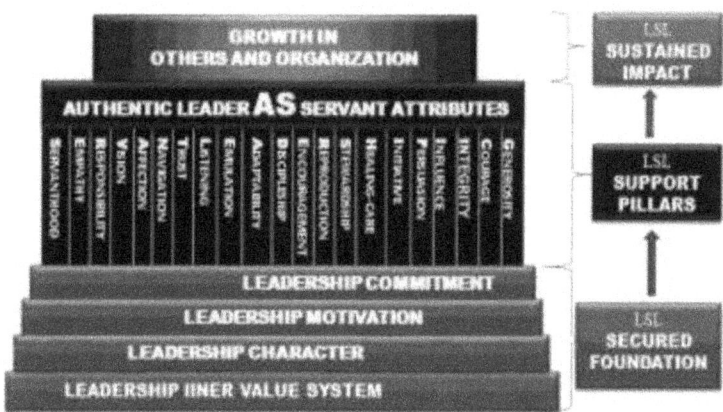

Figure 1.2: Servant leadership outward attributes (dark blue) and relationship to four foundational layers of the LSL Model

Figure 1.2 shows that the leader's attributes are shaped and secured by his four foundational layers (leadership inner value system, leadership character, motivation, and commitment). The attributes of the leader–servants are also conceptualized as the support pillars that will establish and support the personal authenticity of the leader, what the leader, does and the effectiveness of the leadership process. Thus, the attributes represent functional pillars of authentic leadership that can be learned or enriched as described in detail in the subsequent chapters. The combined effect of a secured foundation and stable

COMPARISONS WITH OTHER WORKS

support pillars will make a sustained impact on the growth of followers and the organization.

The original works by Greenleaf (1970) in servant leadership [1] have been reviewed by Larry Spears (1996), who identified listening, empathy, healing, awareness, persuasion, conceptualization, foresight, stewardship, commitment to the growth of others, and building community as the ten distinguishing characteristics of servant leadership. [2] Russell (2001) has studied these attributes and have shown them to be essential in servant leadership and concluded that these qualities generally "grow out of the inner values and beliefs of individual leaders." [3] Russell and Stone (2002) extended the Greenleaf 10 attributes to 20 attributes observed in servant-leaders. These 20 attributes were categorized by these authors as either functional attributes (intrinsic characteristics of servant-leaders) or accompanying attributes (complement attributes that enhance the functional attributes).[4] The operational attributes were identified as vision, honesty, integrity, trust, modeling, service, pioneering, appreciation, and empowerment with the accompanying attributes of communication, credibility, competence, stewardship, visibility, influence, persuasion, listening, encouragement, teaching, and delegation. Only three of the attributes identified by Greenleaf were identified, and all three were accompanying attributes rather than functional. Responsibility, adaptability, affection, discipleship, navigation, and reproduction attributes which are considered critical in biblical-based servant leadership in my LSL model are not covered by Russell and Greenleaf. As shown in the description of the attributes in Table 1.2, most of the attributes reported by Russell and Stone (2002)[5] or Greenleaf [1] can be seen either in the twenty attributes or their associated characteristics. Integrity and honesty for example are leadership characteristics of trust and other attributes rather than an independent attributes. I take the position that servant leadership attributes are functional attributes in acts of duty to others and emanate from the inner value system of the leader.

CHAPTER 1
UNDERSTANDING LEADERSHIP ATTRIBUTES

Table 1.2: Description of the functional leader-servant outward leadership attributes and associated principles and characteristics

Leader–Servant Leadership Attributes	Principles of Leadership Attributes	Leadership Characteristics
Affection: *This is the combined love-based works toward providing the essential help or services for the spiritual growth or survival of another person. .* (Chapter 2)	*Affection flows from a person to produce positive emotions for the well-being of another person*	Kindness Compassion Practical Love Affective signs Appreciation
Discipleship: *This is the combined acts of personally developing, intentionally equipping, and attentively empowering growth in others to reproduce a heart of service.* (Chapter 3)	*Discipleship transforms and empowers followers for service leadership that grows communities.*	Inspiring Shepherding Equipping Developing Empowering
Emulation: *This is the combined acts of initiating an authentic servant attitude as a model of service worthy of following* (Chapter 4)	*A great leader-servant outwardly and positively inspires a pattern of good works for others to follow.*	Inspiration Motivation Initiation Model Following
Generosity: *This is the combined acts of freely sharing with and giving to others as an act of kindness, without expectation of reward or return to him.* (Chapter 5)	*Generosity is an outward measure of the level of sacrifice, what is shared, or the impact a giving makes, not just the size of the giving.*	Sharing Giving Kindness Affection Love
Healing-Care: *This is the combined acts of providing comfort and empathy to make others whole emotionally and spiritually along with tending to the follower's physical and mental well-being.* (Chapter 6)	*Comforting others in any trouble with the comfort with which we are comforted by God, brings healing - wholeness.*	Self-Healing Empathy Reconciliation Comfort Relational
Influence: *This is the combined acts of positively affecting desired change in conduct,*	*The true measure of leadership success in affecting*	Model Positive attitude Authority

performance, and relational connections toward others-centered course of action or service. (Chapter 7)	desired change in conduct, performance, and relational connections in others is influence	Connection Wisdom Intelligence,
Persuasion: This is the combined acts of communicating perspective to connect, challenge, and convince with a compelling purpose to convert others to a new position. (Chapter 8)	The means of transforming others to a new perspective is through empathetic persuasion	Connecting Challenging Communicating Convincing Converting Encouraging
Reproduction: This is the combined acts of developing your leadership qualities in others and releasing them as successors to continue a greater mission. (Chapter 9)	Great leaders produce successors for legacy and greater courses as an expected product of an effective leadership reproduction.	Selecting Mentoring Equipping Empowering Releasing
Servanthood: This is the combined acts of humility, willingness, and intentionality in service to others through selfless sacrifice and submission as a servant. (Chapter 10)	A leader-servant is most qualified to lead when most ready to serve as a servant for the growth of others. The role of a leader is to serve as a servant	Servant's heart Humility Sacrifice Service Willingness Submissiveness
Trust: This is the combined acts of positive display of character, competence, credibility, and shared relational connections that produce assured trust-confidence of the trustee in the trusted. (Chapter 11)	True leadership trust produces assured trustee's confidence and readiness to follow based on the credibility, competence, and shared relational connections of the trusted.	Character Competence Integrity Credibility Confidence

PRINCIPLE OF LEADERSHIP ATTRIBUTE

In the context of servant leadership, a leadership attribute is a level above the leadership characteristic or trait of a leader. The principle of leadership attribute states that every leadership attribute has a set of distinguishing characteristics that make up the inward or outward display of the attribute. The principle reflects the essential designed purpose or outcome of the attribute or the inevitable consequence of the effective practice of the attribute. Thus, the principle of leadership attribute is a concise statement about the fundamental truth, value, or belief about the attribute in a leadership situation; it is a statement that establishes an idea about the outcome of the attribute for guiding the practical application of the attribute and its characteristics. I will postulate and frame each principle as an additive function of the characteristics of the attribute. A statement of each principle is quoted at the beginning or below the title of each chapter. It is yet to be experimentally proven if the attribute is a linear or some other non-linear function of these characteristics as variables. It is expected, however, that each character will contribute to the effectiveness of the attribute in varying degrees.

AUTHENTIC LEADERSHIP ATTRIBUTES

At a personal level, attributes are the value-based inside-out moral leadership assets that can be related to the authenticity of a leader-servant. The complexity of defining authenticity has been noted in the literature. The subject of authentic leadership is well covered in the works of Terry (1993),[5] George (2003),[6] and Shair and Eilam (2005).[7] All appear to agree that authenticity requires self-awareness and objective self-identity in personal and social interactions with others. In his book, *Advocacy Leadership*, Professor Gary L. Anderson offers individual, organizational, and societal perspectives on authenticity: "Authenticity, at a peculiar level, is living a life, whether in the private or professional term. This is congruent with one's espoused values; at the structural level, authenticity has to do with viewing human beings as ends in themselves, rather than means to other ends; at the public level, it is a state of affairs that is congruous with the shared political and cultural values of society." [8]

The basic tenets of these perspectives are very fitting to authenticity as a qualifying element of leader-servant leadership attributes. The attribute reflects how the followers see the leader based on the leader's distinctive features displayed through his or her actions personally, organizationally, and societally. The leader is seen as a leader-servant or serving leader because the followers see him lead as a servant from an inside-out value of others. This is what makes the leader authentic. Authenticity means that what a leader displays outside, in personal or leadership life of service to others, and society is based on the values the leader espouses inside.

Authenticity in servant leadership can be one or two types or both: *Outbound Authenticity and Outward Authenticity*: The Outbound (outward-bound) Authenticity is the genuineness of personal honesty from your inner strength and abilities; what you say and how you act emanate from who you are or how you feel inside. It reflects the essential truth and honesty about your outward-bound inner strength.

Outward authenticity, on the other hand, describes the truthfulness of your credibility and honesty displayed outward in relation to others; your *outer* visible behavior or how you act outwardly towards others reflects exactly your true intentions.

While *outward* authenticity is the visible *outer* indicator of the truth of who you are inside, *outbound* authenticity is outward-bound attribute from the inside of who you are. Credibility in this context is the influence a leader has to attract believability, trustworthiness, and authenticity; it is the believability, trustworthiness, and authenticity of who you are inside and outside.

A key element of personal authenticity is that it is seen or measured in the context of societal, cultural, and organizational interactions. In that context, achieving individual authenticity becomes a challenge since it is influenced by social factors and dispositions of individuals who usually depend on liberal and organizational realities. However, for leader-servant leadership, the leader can face those changing times by remaining focused on his key Biblical-based principles or *Leadership Inner Value System*. Thus, I am interested in authenticity as an essential element of effective Leader-servant leadership attributes or Leader-servant leadership attributes as drivers of leadership authenticity. With that in mind, the first critical element of authenticity in practicing or developing efficient leader-servant leadership attributes is inside-out self-examination relative to the people served rather than the organization. You may ask yourself: What will be my response when the people I lead act or react in a certain way, will it be negative or positive? What are my strengths and vulnerabilities at those times?

CHAPTER 1
UNDERSTANDING LEADERSHIP ATTRIBUTES

Professor Yacobi in his post, "Elements of Human Authenticity," noted that since "the self -arise attribute emerges from interactions between self, others, and the environment in a complex society and world, there may co-exist multiple complicated identities depending on place and context." [9] He went on to identify the following <u>essential elements of personal authenticity</u>: self-awareness, unbiased self-examination, accurate self-knowledge, reflective judgment, personal responsibility, and integrity, genuineness, and humility, empathy for others, understanding of others, optimal utilization of feedback from others. All of these are covered under the leadership attributes or characteristics shown in Table 1.2.

Bill George, in his book, *Authentic Leadership*, takes the position that to be an authentic leader; a person must have the following essential characteristics: [10]

- Behavior based on value: He must understand his own values and exhibit behavior to others based on those values;
- He must not compromise his values in difficult situations but could use the situation to strengthen personal values in those situations.
- Passion from a clear purpose: Be self-aware of who he is, where he is going, and the right thing to do.
- Compassion from the heart: He must lead from a compassionate heart that allows them to be sensitive to the plight and needs of others,
- Connectedness from a relationship; he must be relationally connected with people he leads,
- Consistency from the self-disciple: He must demonstrate self-discipline to remain calm, collected, and consistent in a stressful situation.

Modeled after the elements above, Table 1.3 lists six essential characteristics of authenticity for servant leadership. These fundamental characteristics cover the five identified above and can also be aligned with the leadership characteristics in Table 1.2. Each attribute in Table 1.2 is expected to pass the personal authenticity test in Tables 1.3, 1.4. In a survey of 132 Christian leaders, seventy-four percent (74%) of them agreed that they always or frequently exhibit servant leadership attributes. [11] Thus, a pass of the outward authenticity test means that a pure leader must demonstrate 70% or more of these essential elements of this legitimacy. (That is, 70% YES in the assessment questions in Tables 1.3, 1.4).

It needs to be noted, however, that a secular leader could be authentic and still lack some of the essential servant leadership attributes or characteristics such as selflessness, servanthood, and love-motivated servant attitudes of a leader-servant. Effective leader-servants are authentic leaders and personal authenticity is an essential element of leader-servant leadership. The key test for leader-servant authenticity is the quality of his inside-out value and personal character. What is most important is a change from the inside-out.

	Table 1.3: The test of essential elements of personal inner strength authenticity in servant leadership		
	Elements of Inner Strength Authenticity	**Inner Strength (Outbound) Authenticity Assessment Questions**	**YES / NO**
1	Personal inside-out value-based behavior	Are your personal inside-out values aligned with acts of service and behavior outside?	1
		Are you honest to yourself in relation to your inner strengths and abilities?	2
2	Inside-out Self-Awareness	Do you have unbiased self-examination, and accurate self-knowledge of who you are inside-out?	3
		Do you know your inner strength and weaknesses in relation to the good you want to show as an outward attribute?	4
3	Inside-out Empathy-Compassion	Do you know and feel from your inside what you want for your followers?	5
		Are you motivated to empathize, based on your inside feelings?	6
4	Inside-out Connection with followers	Do you feel deep, personal, and spiritual connection with your followers?	7
		Does what you say and how you act reflect how you feel when you relate to others?	8
5	Inside-out Emotional Self-regulation	Do you have difficulty controlling your emotion in order to remain calm in a stressful situation?	9
		Are you always able to comfort yourself?	10
6	Inside-out Authenticity Feedback	Do your followers see your inside-out value from your outside behavior?	11
		Will your followers feel that what you say you are is congruent with how you act?	12
	#YESs_____ ; # NOs_____ : Outbound Authenticity: YES/ 12————%		

CHAPTER 1
UNDERSTANDING LEADERSHIP ATTRIBUTES

Table 1.4: The test of essential elements of personal outward authenticity in servant leadership			
	Elements of Personal Outward Authenticity	Personal Outward Authenticity Assessment Questions	YES or NO
1	Personal value-based outward behavior	Are your personal values and beliefs aligned with your acts of service and behavior toward others?	1
		Do you live out your life according to your beliefs?	2
2	Personal Self-Awareness	Do you have clarity of your personal vision and purpose?	3
		Does what you know about yourself accurately describe what others say?	4
3	Personal Outward Empathy-Compassion	Do you apply how you feel to what your followers need?	5
		Do you lead from a compassionate heart and are you sensitive to the plight and needs of others?	6
4	Personal Connection with followers	Do you feel deep, personal connection with your followers?	7
		Does your outward action toward others reflect exactly your true intentions?	8
5	Outward Emotional Self-regulation	Do you have difficulty controlling your emotions to remain calm in a stressful situation?	9
		Does your evaluation of your value of others agree with how valued they feel?	10
6	Personal Authenticity Feedback	Do your followers see your outward acts as true and honest?	11
		Can your followers see other-centeredness in 70% or more of your attributes?	12
#YESs_____ ; # NOs_____ ; Outward Authenticity: YES/ 12---------%			

Table 1.5. Leader As Servant-Leadership Audit

A servant-leader in his leadership position purposefully choses to serve and inspire acts of service in others by his example. Select and circle best answer to questions
1=Never; 2=Almost never; 3=Sometimes; 4=Frequently; 5 =Always

	Servant Leadership assessment questions	Circle no
1	I am willing and other-centered, and readily chose to serve others as a servant for their personal growth	1 2 3 4 5
2	I model others-centered attitude in my service and relationships and inspire same for others to follow	1 2 3 4 5
3	I have a sense of obligation, willingness, and accountability for the service towards others	1 2 3 4 5
4	I have the foresightedness to specify in the present view what others' growth should be in a given future	1 2 3 4 5
5	I work toward providing the essential help or services for the spiritual growth or survival of the others;	1 2 3 4 5
6	I provide the needed purposeful course of action for how to chart the course to for my followers.	1 2 3 4 5
7	I display external credibility and a strong sense of character based on values, beliefs, and competence;	1 2 3 4 5
8	In communication, I attentively perceive and hear what is communicated, reflectively listen to understand and to be understood	1 2 3 4 5
9	I walk through with others in their state (suffering, emotions, etc.) in a way that provides the needed care and well-being	1 2 3 4 5
10	I have a measure of self-secured flexibility to adapt appropriate attitude to serve all people in different situations	1 2 3 4 5
11	I personally develop, intentionally equip, and attentively nurture spiritually growth in others	1 2 3 4 5
12	My act of bravery instills in others the courage and confidence to follow or persevere in a course of action	1 2 4 5
13	I develop my leadership qualities in others as successors to continue in a purposeful mission	1 2 3 4 5
14	I manage, maintain,, and account for all resources entrusted to me and being responsible for the difference my acts make	1 2 3 4 5
15	As a care-giver, I act to comfort and make others whole emotionally	1 2 3 4 5
16	When I see a need, I originate a vision and action, and stay committed to meet that need and desired change	1 2 3 4 5

Chapter 1
Understanding Leadership Attributes

17	I display a holistic view of an issue to inform, transform or convert others to my view through empathetic persuasion	1	2	3	4	5
18	I freely share what I have sacrificially as an act of kindness to others, without expectation of reward in return	1	2	3	4	5
19	My act of influence is to affect the actions, behavior, opinions, etc., of others based on trust, credibility and relationship	1	2	3	4	5
20	In the face challenges and danger, I act with bravery to overcome fear and take a stand with strength and conviction	1	2	3	4	5
Score Range	Add up the numbers in each column (Total Score____ Check and Understand the key areas to work on					
81-100	Strong Leader-Servant; keep it up, go and train others.					
66-80	Above average Leader-Servant; work 25% of key areas					
50-65	Average but developing; need to work on 50% of key areas					
34-49	Below average leader; work on 75% of key areas					
<34	Not a Leader-Servant; need training in all areas					

Summary 1
Understanding Leadership Process

Before starting this exercise, please read and follow the instruction in the preface of this workbook. Answers to these questions are contained in this chapter. Completion of these exercises after reading the chapter should take 60-90 minutes.

Discovering the Leadership Attributes

1. What is your alternative definition of leadership? In learning to lead, how would you differentiate the following elements:
    a. Leadership,
    b. Leader as servant leadership.
    c. Leadership characteristics.
    d. Leadership attributes
2. What are the key differences between the Leader as Servant and the Servant as Leader Leadership philosophies?
3. What was the original source of the Servant as Leader (SL)?

4. What is the key framework of a Leader as a Servant Leadership?
5. Authenticity in servant leadership can be one or two types or both *Outbound Authenticity and Outward Authenticity*: Describe a time when you displayed:
    a. The Outbound (outward-bound)— *outbound* authenticity is outward-bound attribute from the inside of who you are.
    b. *The Outward Authenticity*—*outward* authenticity is the visible *outer* indicator of the truth of who you are inside,
6. Describe the key elements of personal authenticity seen or measured in the context of societal, cultural, and organizational interactions.
7. How are the essential characteristics of authentic leader in leadership process in challenging times.
8. How much of a leader-servant are you? Take the personal leader-servant audit in Table 1.5.
9. Based on the questions in Table 1.5, can you identify each of the twenty attributes? What ones did you score 3 ("sometimes") or less than 3?

CHAPTER 2
INFLUENCE LEADERSHIP ATTRIBUTE

The true measure of leadership success in affecting desired change in conduct, perfomance, and relational connections in others is influence

Leadership is an integrative process in which a person applies appropriate (leadership) attributes to guide and influence the desired attitudinal changes in others toward accomplishing a particular goal. When he asked top CEOs what prompted them to become leaders, John C. Maxwell the author of 21 Irrefutable Laws of Leadership found that 85% said they were "influenced by another leader," compared to 10% and 5% for "natural gifting" and "result of a crisis," respectively

When we consider influence as a servant leadership attribute, we are talking about a distinguishing leadership characteristic that displays on the outside what a leader is inside, influence takes on a deeper meaning. In this chapter, I will biblically and from research, explore and identify the key leadership characteristics of influence, and like in other chapters, frame definitions of the Servant-Leadership influence attribute and principle. Based on those characteristics, I will discuss the key outcomes of effective leadership influence attributes and frame those as the principle of leadership influence attributes. The chapter presents in detail how a leader-servant can develop those characteristics and then effectively practice service leadership.

CHARACTERISTICS OF INFLUENCE ATTRIBUTE

Influencers command authority to influence others to follow their lead. The Bible includes several examples of leaders of influence. When Jesus called His disciples to follow Him, what swayed them to obey to follow without hesitation? "Then He said to them, 'Follow Me, and I will make you fishers of men.'" They immediately left their nets and followed Him" (Matt 4:19-20). By "follow me", Jesus was telling them: "come after me," "come to receive my doctrines," "imitate me," and "be my disciples in every respect." These ordinary fishermen minding their fishing businesses were quick to abandon all to follow Jesus. Why? It's possible that Jesus looked authoritative and different from them, with some display of personality of importance, and by the way; he commanded them. Another likely explanation could be that He could influence them to follow Him based on his divine *power and authority*.

Influencers are *independent thinkers*. Joshua and Caleb distinguished themselves as influencers. Twelve people as leaders in their tribes were sent out to spy on the land God had promised to give them. All twelve received the same instructions and promise, and all were exposed to identical opportunities. However, the twelve returned from the mission with different reports: The majority (ten) allowed the challenges they saw to cloud their vision of the power of God and completely misunderstood their purpose. Out of fear, they saw themselves as grasshoppers compared to the inhabitants of the place and reported that they could not go possess the land. In contrast, Joshua and Caleb distinguished themselves as independent thinkers. They understood the power of God in light of the challenges ahead in possessing the Promised Land, saw the opportunities despite challenges, and understood their purpose in the mission.

Influencers display *passion and convictions*. This attitude allowed them, Joshua and Caleb to speak passionately on faith out of a conviction of the power of God without fear (Numbers 14:6-9). Joshua and Caleb influenced the people to go. The result was that Joshua and Caleb lived on to enter the Promised Land, while the ten perished in the wilderness with the rest of that generation.

A positive attitude make influence effective. What was the major difference between these two groups in influencing the desired behavior? A positive attitude! Positive attitude born of conviction is an internal driver of the leadership process of influence. Our attitude often determines the difference between our success, failure, and our approach to everything else in life.

Nehemiah demonstrated that the quality of a *negotiator* is a part of influence. His capacity to negotiate through action allowed him to chart the course of action to influence people's minds to successfully rebuild the broken walls of Jerusalem against all enemies. Several lessons on influence can be learned from Nehemiah's example: He was careful to map out a course of action to rebuild. He negotiated his actions through the people by identifying with the people. He carefully assessed the situation and took it upon himself to originate the process of rebuilding. The initiative to rebuild to remove the reproach of the burned gates and ruins of Jerusalem became his own burden. In the operation, he proceeded to engage key people to help him influence the desired change (Nehemiah Chapters 1 and 2). Several critical influence initiation lessons can be learned from Nehemiah: He first worked on understanding what was at stake and walking along with God for empowerment and self-motivation for action. His knowledge of what he learned further influenced his self-determination and will have to initiate the action. He identified and approached the key people of influence and received permission, resources, and support to rebuild. He met with his followers, educated them, and cast the vision to build the needed synergy for rebuilding. He educated them on the benefits of rebuilding before discussing what was required from them for buy-in. He encouraged the people in order to receive a unified consensus for the initiation. He assessed and understood the situation but acted quietly, planning the project and avoiding distractions and unwanted advice.

Influencers connect well with people. In addition to Nehemiah's example above and his ability to connect with the people, Apostle Paul stands as another example. As a great leader whose mission was to spread the gospel, Paul instructed Timothy to consider key steps in establishing leaders in the church (1 Timothy 5:17-25). He recommended the following steps: Identify and select those with character, gifts, and influence. The Apostle Paul knew from his own leadership that influences attributes were key to his success in the changes for which he hoped in the new churches he planted. What was it about Paul throughout his ministry that was successful in propagating the Gospel and affecting believers everywhere he went, even today, with his message? Among Paul's great assets was his ability to connect with his audience in person and mind-to-mind, through prayers and in letters—that allowed his audience to walk the same walk with him. He empathetically and persuasively communicated to connect and convert people to the Gospel message. He was very adaptable and knew how to abase himself to communicate his purpose to anyone. He was an authentic teaching leader with the power of influence through his words, some borne out of personal life experiences. He used those experiences in empathy to walk along with his audience to connect.

Other common characteristic's traits of highly influential people include wisdom, charisma, intelligence, love, power, and several others summarized in Table 7. The list includes, but is not limited to, characteristics identified and supported by other authors. [33,34] Clearly, these characteristics are generally shared as outcomes of effective leadership attributes. They support John C. Maxwell's notion that a "True measure of leadership is influence." [35] Some of these are innate in nature, while others are developed intentionally by a leader concerning serving others.

Table 7: Characteristics of Positively Influential Leader-Servants

Positively Influential Leader-Servants are......			
1	Consistent	18	Followed/Modeled
2	Intentional	19	Initiators
3	Focused	20	Transparent
4	Generous	21	Competitive
5	Passionate	22	Negotiators
6	Servants	23	Insightful
7	Courageous	24	Motivators
8	Respected	25	Learners
9	Communicative	26	Teachable
10	Relational	27	Mission-driven
11	Trustworthy	28	Humble
12	Engaging	29	Credible
13	Loving	30	Intelligent
14	Charismatic	31	Powerful
15	Knowledgeable/Wise	32	Optimistic
16	Authoritative/Bold	33	Visionary
17	Honest/ have Integrity	34	Ethical

PRINCIPLE OF LEADERSHIP INFLUENCE ATTRIBUTE

Although the majority of these characteristics have been discussed or included in other leadership attributes or characteristics, the key distinguishing characteristics of the Servant-Leadership influence attribute are the positive attitude, modeling, authority, and connection. Based on the identified leadership characteristic, a functional definition is framed as:

Servant leadership influence attribute is the combined acts of positively affecting desired change in conduct, performance, and relational connections toward the others-centered course of action or service.

The primary act of influence attributed to affect a change in something (actions, behaviors, opinions, etc.) is a positive display of certain characteristics of the leader toward others. All effective influencers sway people's disposition to a new action or behavior toward a specific desired outcome; this leads me to the following Servant-Leadership influence principle:

The true measure of leadership success in affecting desired change in conduct, performance, and relational connections in others is influence

Leadership influence attribute is displayed through the model, connections, and authority of the leader to affect a change in others. This is illustrated in Figure 7 and expressed as an additive law as:

INFLUENCE = MODEL + AUTHORITY + CONNECTION

SUMMARY 2
INFLUENCE LEADERSHIP ATTRIBUTE

Before starting this exercise, please read and follow the instruction in the preface of this workbook. Answers to these questions are contained in this chapter. Completion of these exercises after reading the chapter should take 60-90 minutes.

Discovering Influence Leadership Attribute

1. What is influence in the context of servant leadership attribute?
2. What does the bible teach about?
3. What are the distinguishing Characteristics of Influence leadership Attribute?
4. How did Jesus demonstrate influence leadership (Matt 4:19-20)?
5. Influencers display *passion and convictions*. How did Joshua and Caleb display those qualities (Numbers 14:6-9)?
6. Nehemiah demonstrated that the quality of a *negotiator* as part of influence leadership attribute. How was this important in his work (Nehemiah Chapters 1 and 2).
7. What other common characteristics of highly influential people have you observed in yourself or people

Understanding the Principle of Influence leadership attribute

1. The key distinguishing characteristics of the Servant-Leadership influence attribute are the positive attitude, modeling, authority, and connection. Define i*nfluence leadership attribute*
2. State Servant-Leadership influence principle.
3. State the additive law of influence leadership attribute

Practicing Influence-Attribute

1. What would you consider the key characteristics of influence leadership attributes?
2. How many acts of influence as an attribute do you display?

CHAPTER 3
DEVELOPING THE INFLUENCE-MODEL

The influence model is the pattern of behaviors or the approach you desire to see in others. This includes models such as leading by example, walking the talk, adopting a Christ-like pattern that followers can understand and follow, negotiating your thoughts with people, and being fervent for the convictions in your beliefs without lording it over others. We can develop influence-model abilities by the following actions: Inform and transform to influence, model influence with the assets w have, be bold and passionate in our convictions, and influence from values and spiritual presence.

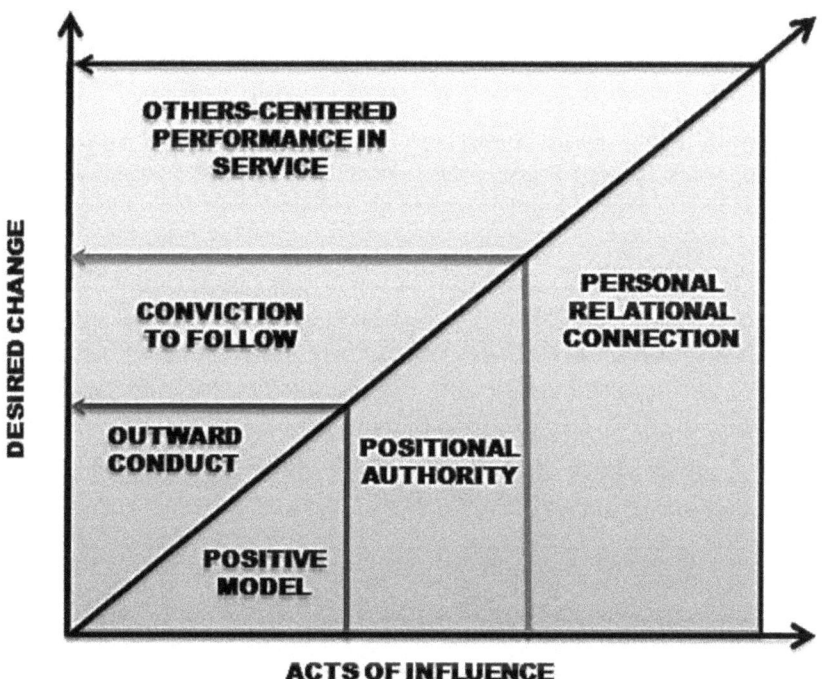

Figure 7. Servant leadership influence-attribute model

Inform and Transform to Influence.

Trans-formative influencers readily share patterns and steps that followers can follow. The goal is not only to inform them but to transform their minds toward desired change. Trans-formative influencers build others up by empowering them with new information. He uses the information shared as a catalyst for change. The expected outcome of the influence is for the individual to develop the characteristics that God can use. Jesus taught his followers that they were the light and salt of the world; maintaining their shine and flavor was needed spiritual conditioning for the Kingdom's businessmen. Jesus said, "You are the light of the world. A city on a hill cannot be hidden" (Matthew 5:14, NIV). This means that the life of trans-formative influencers and who they are to God should influence others to give glory to God. The transformation may also include influencing change to help followers arise in their profession or spiritual growth.

MODELING INFLUENCE WITH YOUR ASSETS

What are your strengths and interests that can help build up others? Think about the Apostle Paul. For others to have an encounter with Jesus and for them to know Him was Paul's main inspiration and motivation for writing the Epistles. His inspired works are the second-most impacting piece of writing after the words of Jesus that speaks directly to the heart of humanity. Such writings came from a man who had many challenges of his own that he called thorns in his flesh. He suffered so much for the Gospel, and yet you could always feel the diligence and industrious attitude of this servant. Most influencers I know directly or through the study are very diligent and hardworking and use what they know or do best to influence others. Some of the most effective change agents for black males are athletes who are the best in their field. They are the best motivators for young kids who look up to them for inspiration.

INFLUENCE FROM PASSION AND CONVICTIONS

When you start and listen to any influencer—from Jesus Christ to Martin Luther King— one thing is very common: the passion and boldness with which the message is delivered. It is like listening to a medical doctor share information about a new life-changing drug that will cure a sickness you have. You simply see in the message that the messenger believes in the message and that what you are hearing will change your situation. There are self-confidence and assuredness with conviction in what they are saying. This is why motivational speakers are great influencers. Show me any mega-congregation, and I will show you a bold, passionate influencer as the leading pastor. Such influencers passionately and enthusiastically deliver facts you know in order to show you things you never thought before or imagined might be possible.

INFLUENCE FROM YOUR SPIRITUAL PRESENCE

A leader's use of the respect he gains from his moral character can be very effective in not only influencing individuals but gathering people together. To influence respect in their environment, influencers are humble, have value, and respect all people. They also influence desired behavior by representing godliness to transform the environment's supernatural presence. The nearness of a transcendent leader in any gathering of people presents an aroma of influence and spiritual light. The mere presence of a man or woman of God in a gathering positively affects people's actions and reactions. Jesus, in stilling the storm, transformed the immediate environment and filled the atmosphere with God's love, joy, peace, and patience.

SUMMARY 3
DEVELOPING THE INFLUENCE-MODEL

Before starting this exercise, please read and follow the instruction in the preface of this workbook. Answers to these questions are contained in this chapter. Completion of these exercises after reading the chapter should take 60-90 minutes.

Discovering the Influence leadership Model

1. Define the influence model
2. List some of the models or patterns you have adopted in your work as a leader

Practicing Influence-model
1. How can you develop influence-model abilities/
2. What are the goals of transformative influencers in sharing patterns and steps that followers can follow?
3. With respect to influence-model, what did Jesus mean when He said, "You are the light of the world. A city on a hill cannot be hidden" (Matthew 5:14, NIV).
4. How can influence be modeled with your assets (strength and interest)?
5. Influence from Passion with convictions is common among
6. influencer—from Jesus Christ to Martin Luther King. How is that true mega-congregation,
7. How can leaders Influence from spiritual presence?

Influence-Model is the example or pattern of behavior or approaches you desire to see in others.
1. Give three such examples in your life.
2. Explain how you can influence someone to be Christ-like.

CHAPTER 4
DEVELOPING THE INFLUENCE-AUTHORITY

Influence-authority is any action taken based on the positional authority or expertise a person holds to build others' confidence to affect a change. This includes actions such as being bold and passionate when it matters; exercising authority; having conviction, expertise, and negotiation skills; exhibiting confidence to change by using encouragement; and using consistent or authoritative facts. For example:

INFLUENCE BY AUTHORITY WITH CONVICTION

In many instances when presidents and secretaries of the state make speeches about military action, they present themselves as very bold and passionate about their convictions and position. Examples include Bush on the Iraqi war and Secretary of State John Kerry on defending a deal to curb Iran's nuclear program in exchange for limited sanctions. Alternatively, Martin Luther King, Jr's bold and passionate "I Have a Dream" speech was based on his convictions regarding the state of race in America. In each of these cases, these leaders were backed by their authority (position, expertise, or information they have).

ENCOURAGING AND INSPIRING CONFIDENCE

An important characteristic of encouragement includes reassuring someone with the courage or confidence to follow a new course of action. This means that leaders can influence followers by uplifting them with these attributes toward the actions needed for desired change. One of the tools Paul and Barnabas used to affect changes in the lives of early Christians was the encouragement to remain genuine to the Gospel message. Joseph, who was also named Barnabas (meaning, "Son of Encouragement") said: "Then when he had come and witnessed the grace of God, he rejoiced and began to encourage them all with resolute heart to remain true to the Lord; for he was a good man...And considerable numbers were brought to the Lord" (Acts 11:23-24, NIV). The encouragement influenced the unbelievers to believe and be converted. Those who were converted were also encouraged and disciplined to become strong and remain in the faith. The inspiration attitude came from Barnabas, who also mentored Paul and encouraged him to join them in Antioch. The number of believers grew, and the result was that; "the disciples were first called Christians at Antioch" (Acts 11:23-26, NIV).

DISCRETE USE OF AUTHORITY TO INFLUENCE

Exercise of one authority over others remains the most direct and immediate action to influence change in an authoritarian-type leadership process. Here, we have seen the truth in the saying that "absolute power corrupts absolutely." In the Leader as Servant Leadership process, "authority" is very discrete and often reflexive in the sense that authority is instinctive, not lorded over on the people, but specifically and instinctively directed. Jesus was an authority. However, He discretely exercised that authority when he had to. Most of the time, He influenced change in people when they recognized his authority and responded naturally to his teachings. Jesus could have shown His authority and power when he was arrested. In contrast, Peter exercised power in an authoritarian sense by drawing his sword and cutting off the high priest's servant's right ear during Jesus' arrest. Jesus was prudent in the use of his authority here. He touched the servant's ear and healed it because Paul's bold, imprudent action could have endangered the lives of all the disciples in the hands of the soldiers (Luke 22:50-52). Christ chose to be passive and use his authority discretely; he had the power to defend himself without Peter drawing his sword; if it was necessary, he could have had His Father send more than twelve legions of angels. However, that would have been contrary to the nature of His kingdom and executing His Father's will. As a leader-servant, Jesus readily gave up authority because of the change. He wanted to influence what was much more important to God than the immediate pride and honor of Peter and others fighting to protect Him with the human sword.

Of course, we have seen cases where the same power and authority have been used negatively to influence people to do the wrong things or oppress others; naturally, power has the tendency to be crooked. When power is incumbent and unchallenged, only in one person or group, it becomes absolute power and will invariably pervert. Hitler, for example, was the highest dictatorial authority in Germany at his time; he became evil and corrupt because no one who loved his life dared to challenge him.

PURPOSEFUL USE OF FACTS TO INFLUENCE CHANGE

Effective use of information and facts is an authoritative pathway to convert people to a new idea or option. This was the challenge the Apostles and Paul faced in establishing the early churches in Rome, Corinth, Antioch, and other parts of the world. The Bible is the authoritative and authentic Word of God, and no book has ever been written nor will be written that influences people's lives as profoundly. Why? It is based on irrefutable facts about God's dealings in creation, the fall of man due to sin, and salvation and redemption and reconciliation of man to God through Jesus Christ. The disciples and the Apostles used these facts to change their worlds. Believers today are reaching the uttermost corners of the world with the same unchanging message.

We also see throughout secular history how people have used facts—good or bad—to influence change. General Colin Powell, as U.S. Secretary of State under George Bush, combined facts he knew or assumed to be true at the time with passion and boldness in presenting those facts to influence people's voting action to authorize the war in Iraq. Our judicial system influences action on the laws based on lawyers' correct use of facts to build their cases.

SUMMARY 4
DEVELOPING THE INFLUENCE-AUTHORITY

Before starting this exercise, please read and follow the instruction in the preface of this workbook. Answers to these questions are contained in this chapter. Completion of these exercises after reading the chapter should take 60-90 minutes.

Define influence-authority

1. Influence-authority with conviction where and when it matters.
2. Influenced backed by authority can be observed when leaders (presidents and secretaries of the state of nations) make speeches about military action: how has authority with conviction influenced change where and when it matters? .
3. An important characteristic of encouragement includes reassuring someone with the courage or confidence to follow a new course of action. How can leaders influence change through encouragement?

Practicing Influence-authority

1. How did Paul and Barnabas use acts of encouragement to influence change? (Acts 11:23-26, NIV); what was the direct outcome of this ac0?).
2. How can a leader use of authority to influence
3. How did Jesus and Peter use authority to influence change (Luke 22:50-52).
4. Purposeful use of facts to influence change
5. Effective use of information and facts is an authoritative pathway to convert people to a new idea or option. Why has the Bible proven to be authoritative in influencing change more than any book even written that influences people's lives

Influence-Authority is any action taken based on the positional authority or expertise to build the confidence of others to affect a change.

1. When was the last time you as a leader or a leader you know influence a desired change in you by his or her life?
2. What did you do and what was the exact impact?
3. What are three strategic actions for influence –authority?

CHAPTER 5
DEVELOPING INFLUENCE-CONNECTION

Influence-connection actions are specific actions taken to influence a desired change in actions or relational behaviors of others. The primary purpose of Paul's writing was to communicate the Gospel message to influence behaviors toward Christ-like living or train others to do the same. Epistle Paul was very masterful in being passionately transparent, authentic, and consistent in his words and actions. He stayed on the message without wavering, even at the risk of appearing repetitious in his message of Christ's death and resurrection as the remedy for sin. Strategic connections that influence change can be developed following these examples:

BUILDING CONNECTIONS TO INFLUENCE

Paul's reasons, as demonstrated through his writing in the openings and endings of his letters with passionate greetings, were mainly to connect with the people before delivering any message. He assures them not of God's love and grace, but his love and care and commitment to their welfare. He prays and thanks God for them and affirms them as much as possible in very specific things. "First, I thank my God through Jesus Christ for all of you, because your faith is being reported all over the world... constantly I remember you in my prayers at all times" (Romans 1:7-10, NIV).

Paul's lavish feelings and concerns affirmed and encouraged them. It is very powerful to hear your leader reassure you of his obligation to your welfare. Paul says; "I am obligated both to Greeks and non-Greeks, both to the wise and the foolish. That is why I am so eager to preach the gospel also to you who are in Rome" (Romans 1:11-15, NIV). This type of connection attitude builds the relationships so critical for any process of influence.

Part of connecting with people is to link them to facts to help them clear any doubts that may hinder their readiness to accept the Gospel. These believers and non-believers knew who Paul used to be—an unbelieving persecutor of believers of the Gospel. However, he tells them he is not ashamed of the Gospel and how God spoke and revealed himself through His creation. To clarify people why the salvation message must be accepted, he shows them the impact of sin on humanity and the gift of God through Jesus Christ. What a way to leave them with no choice but to accept the message! This is an effective influence strategy, almost making them be at his side of experience and the mercy of God through his message.

CONNECTING TO HOPES AND ASPIRATIONS

One of the greatest leaders of our time who influenced his audience by connecting to their hopes and aspirations was Dr. Martin Luther King, Jr. From hopes for civil rights in the 1960s to Brown v. Board of Education and the Rosa Parks incident that culminated in the Birmingham Riots, emerged the birth of a movement and a leader in Dr. King to influence a conversation about change. By all standards, the movement and this influencer represented an era of unprecedented desire for change, including voting rights, equality for all, and the end of oppressive behaviors and discrimination against blacks. With his historic "I have a Dream Speech" on the steps of the Lincoln Memorial, delivered to more than 200,000 people on the Mall, Dr. King effectively connected with people's dreams and aspirations more than anyone had or will ever since Jesus Christ. In the end, he influenced the critical change in the Civil Rights laws of the United States. His statement, "I have a dream that one day on the red hills of Georgia the sons of past slaves, and the sons of former slave owners will be able to sit down with each other at a table of brotherhood" [36] remains a prominent change message that influenced people of different viewpoints to reexamine their positions and come together, if not to all agree, but agree to disagree. To have a black man as a two-term president of the United States says a lot about the progress that has been made and the tremendous influence Dr. King had in American history. A parallel can also be drawn from the case of Nelson Mandela, who over 27 years in prison brought about a change in South Africa. The movie titled

Chapter 5
Developing Influence-Connection

Invictus, released in 2009, portrayed Nelson Mandela's (acted by Morgan Freeman) handling of post-apartheid South Africa as a leader whose major desire was to connect and rebuild a nation that was divided by the evil inflicted by apartheid, through an example of forgiveness and reconciliation. His mindset was for all his people to be free. He recounted this in His book, The Long walk to Freedom,

> "I am not truly free if I am taking away someone else's freedom, just as I am surely not free when my freedom is taken from me. The oppressed and the oppressor alike are robbed of their humanity. When I walked out of prison, that was my mission; to liberate the oppressed and the oppressor." [37]

Mandela's unique ability to care for and connect with individuals around him –friends and former foes-at the personal level is most representative of an influencer; his strategy of connection through the aspirations and hopes of his people was very effective. In one scene in the film, he inquired from one of his security agents how the agent's sick child was getting along. It was very clear in the movie that the security agent felt humbled and connected to the mind and agenda of this president; Mandela cared enough to ask about the agent's unwell child. This was exactly how Jesus exemplified connection-healing care, compassion, and empathy. Connecting with people starts with developing credibility and gaining their trust. The such attitude then allows people to see the leader as an authentic friend or leader-servant. John C. Maxwell's, Law of Connection in his book *21 Irrefutable Law of leadership, posits* that "leaders touch a heart before they ask for a hand." [35] Hence, the first responsibility of a leader as far as influence connection is concerned is to take the intentional step to relate to the hearts and feelings of the followers. The follower will reciprocate, follow, and connect with the leader

MAKING FRIENDS TO CONNECT

It is a lot easier to influence someone who respects you or with whom you are most friendly than someone who does not. However, that respect is earned. To make friends, most influencers are humbly friendly and approachable. Dale Carnegie in his book, *How to Win Friends and Influence People*, argues that success in leadership is based on three primary tenets: Don't criticize, condemn, or complain. [38] These behaviors are self-serving reflections of self-centeredness and egocentric behavior. Instead, leaders should attract people by focusing on what makes others feel significant and by discovering what others find most important. Then, help them meet that need.

VALUING PEOPLE AS ASSETS

Because influencers are themselves influenced and motivated by the progress of the people they serve, they desire to know about the people and how they can best serve them. Influencers are capable of identifying the need and capitalizing on using the assets (gifts, strengths, talents, interests, and uniqueness) of each disciple, subsequently enhancing their ability to grow in their primary talent. The influence attribute allows a leader to assess his followers to understand how they think as part of their accountability to the growth of each person. As stated, people who feel included and valued are more likely to engage in the change process or be open to being influenced toward a desired change.

The diversity of everyone's individual assets defines the strength of the organization. For example, knowing each person's gifts and talents helps the leader better customize the approach that maximizes talent. Needs are deficiencies and weaknesses that must be addressed in training a disciple. Some members may appear talented and mature in skills they have, but are empty spiritually; indeed, that is then their weakness. Some may be spiritual in the wrong doctrine and teaching. Some may confuse religiosity with real Christ-likeness. These flaws must be identified and corrected through sound teaching. How do leaders maximize the followers' talents within a code of conduct that projects a positive reputation to outsiders? The imagery of the flock of God is that of sheep needing care and guidance by the shepherd. The leader must see that the herd is complete, expending 100% effort to ensure that none are lost. This simply means overseeing the work and growth of others as a shepherding leaders.

Former President George H. W. Bush (Papa Bush) will remain in my mind as a leader who counted the value of every nation that mattered when planning the Gulf War with Iraq to build one of the most powerful coalitions since World War II. He built a consensus

CHAPTER 5
DEVELOPING INFLUENCE-CONNECTION

among 34 nations, with differing agendas and desires into one with a unified mission and focus to drive the Iraqi army out of Kuwait. President Bush proved to be an excellent influencer. He lobbied nations one by one according to their interests—security in the region, regional aggression in the Middle East, shared concerns for the European NATO allies, and conflict on the doorstep of Eastern Asian allies. [39] Wikipedia summarized the coalition building this way: "The UN coalition-building efforts were so successful that by the time the fighting (Operation Desert Storm) began on 16 January 1991, twelve countries had sent naval forces, joining the regional states of Saudi Arabia and the Persian Gulf states, as well as the huge array of the U.S. Navy, which deployed six carrier battle groups; eight countries had sent ground forces, joining the regional troops of Bahrain, Kuwait, Oman, Qatar, Saudi Arabia, and the United Arab Emirates, as well as the seventeen heavy and six light brigades of the U.S. Army and nine Marine regiments, with their large support and service forces; and four countries had sent combat aircraft, joining the local air forces of Kuwait, Qatar, and Saudi Arabia, as well as the U.S. Air Force, U.S. Navy, and U.S. Marine aviation, for a grand total of 2,430 fixed-wing aircraft." [39]

SUMMARY 5
DEVELOPING INFLUENCE-CONNECTION

Before starting this exercise, please read and follow the instruction in the preface of this workbook. Answers to these questions are contained in this chapter. Completion of these exercises after reading the chapter should take 60-90 minutes.

Discovering influence-connection

The primary purpose of Paul's writing was to communicate the Gospel message to influence Christ-like living. What were some of pauls influence connection strategy
  1. Strategic connections that influence change can be developed following these examples
  2. Principle of influence-connection

3. John C. Maxwell's, Law of Connection in his book *21 Irrefutable Law of leadership, posits* that "leaders touch a heart before they ask for a hand." [35] What is the first responsibility of a leader as far as influence-connection is concerned?

Principle of Influence-connection

1. In *How to Win Friends and Influence People* [38], what did the author argues were the three primary tenets for success in leadership. And should leaders be the focusing on
2. How can Valuing people as assets be a strategy for influence by connection
3. How did Former President George H. W. Bush (Papa Bush) use this strategy?

Practicing Influence-connection

Influence-connection is a specific connective action taken for the purpose of influencing a desired change in the actions or behaviors of others.

1. Give four examples of how we can develop strategic connections that influence change.
2. What were Paul key strategic actions in building connections to influence, (Romans 1:7-10, NIV). (Romans 1:11-15, NIV).
3. Dr. Martin Luther King, Jr. remain in history as one of the greatest leaders of our time. How did he influence his audience?
4. Nelson Mandela, who over 27 years in prison brought about a change in South Africa. What was the unique quality of this influencer?
5. Where do we start in connecting with people?
6. Take the Leadership Influence attribute audit in Table 6.
7. Based on the questions in Table 6. can you identify each of the acts of influence leadership attribute? What ones did you score 3 ("sometimes") or less than 3? Review and learn and commit to work to improve.

CHAPTER 5
DEVELOPING INFLUENCE-CONNECTION

Table 6.1. Leadership Influence Attribute Audit

Servant leadership influence attribute is the combined acts of positively affecting desired change in conduct, performance, and relational connections toward others-centered course of action or service. Assess the quality of your acts of influence attribute by inserting an X below the number that best describes your response to each statement.

Item	Acts of Influence Attribute Check 1= Always; 2= Frequently; 3= Sometimes; 4= Almost Never; 5= Never	1	2	3	4	5
1	I take specific connective actions to influence desired change in behaviors of others.					
2	I act in positive ways to affect desired change toward others					
3	My influence-model is my pattern of behavior I desire to see in others.					
4	I Inform and transform by sharing patterns and steps that followers can follow					
5	My act of influence transforms minds toward desired change.					
6	**I use** my positional influence or expertise for the purpose of affecting a change.					
7	I inspire followers with confidence toward the actions needed for desired change.					
8	I am usually bold and passionate in my convictions in my acts of influence					
9	I Influence others from my inner values and spiritual presence than by power I have					
10	To influence respect, I am humble, value and respect all people.					
	Add up your rating in each column					
Score Range	Guide and Explanation of Score: understand the areas you need to further develop			Total Score		
10-17	Great Influence Leadership; keep it up!					
18-25	Above Average influencer; need to work on 25% of the areas					
26-33	Average but developing; need to work on 50% of the areas					
34-4	Below average influencer, need to work 75% of the areas					
42-50	No influence leadership ; work in all the areas					

Topic Index

About This Book, 22
Affective Compassion, 73
authentic, 24, 26
authentic leadership, 37
Authentic Leadership, 45
Authenticity, 43
Authoritative Use of Facts, 69, 70
Build connection to Influence, 73
Capitalize on the Assets, 76, 78
Characteristics of Highly Influential People, 57
Comfort, 41
commitment, 19, 25
Comparisons
   with other works, 40
credibility, 48
Discipleship
   definition of, 27
distinguishes
   a leader's act of giving, 29
Functional Definitions, 35
Generosity
   definition of, 29
Generosity c, 29
giving, 29
   habit of, 29
Impact their community, 79
Influence Attribute, 54, 58
Influence- authority, 70
Influence –Connection, 78, 79
INFLUENCE-ATTRIBUTE, 58

influencer, 77
inside-out, 46
Joshua, 19
law of, 42
Leader as Servant Leadership, 42
   definition, 25
Leader First., 23
Leader-as-Servant Leadership, 23
leader-servant's affection-attribute
   definition, 48
leadership, 25
Leadership Attributes, 43
Leadership Inner Value system, 25
Make Friends to Connect, 75
Model, 23
Model Influence, 62
Moses, 19
Navigation-attribute, 48
Organizational leadership trust, 32
Personal Outward Authenticity, 47
Practicing Servant Leadership
   Influence, 59
process, 25
Reconciliation, 84
Servant, 23, 24
test
   for leader-servant authenticity, 46
   of essential elements of personal authenticity, 46, 47
The Leadership Influence-attribute, 41, 57, 79

REFERENCES

[1]Greenleaf, R. (1970). *The Servant as Leader,* Indianapolis: The Robert K. Greenleaf Center

[2]Spears, L. (1996*). "Reflections on Robert K. Greenleaf and servant-leadership."* Leadership & Organization Development Journal, 17(7), 33-35

[3]Russell, R.F. (2001). "The role of values in servant leadership." *Leadership & Organization Development Journal,* 22(2), 76-83

[4]Russell, R.F., and Stone, A.G. (2002). "A review of servant leadership attributes: developing a practical model." *Leadership & Organization Development Journal,* 23(3), 145-15

[5]Terry. R. W (1993*). Authentic Leadership: Courage In Action,* San Francisco, CA ,Jossey-Bass

[6]George, B (2003). *Authentic Leadership: Rediscovering the Secrets to Creating Lasting Value.* San Francisco, CA, Jossey-Bass

[7]Shamir, B. & Eilam, G. (2005). "What's your story? Toward a life-story approach to authentic leadership." Leadership Quarterly, 16, 395–418.

[8]Anderson, GL (2009). Advocacy Leadership: Toward a Post-Reform Agenda in Education, Routledge, New York, 41

[9]Yacobi, B.G. *"Elements of Human Authenticity."* http://www.philosophytogo.org /wordpress/?p=1945, Retrieved, July 15, 2012

[10]George, B (2003). *Authentic Leadership: Rediscovering the Secrets to Creating Lasting Value,* San Francisco, CA, Jossey-Bass

[11]Wosu, SN (2014), *Leader as Servant Leadership Model,* Xulon Press

[33]Brazell, A. "8 Traits of Highly Effective Influencers." http://technosailor.com/2009/03/01/8-traits-of-highly-effective-influencers/10/

[34]Matt Morton (2013). "6 Character Traits that Real Influencers Have in Common." - : http://www.grace-bible.org/resources/blog/6-character-traits-that-real-influencers-have-in-common#sthash.TQIxmxFO.dpuf

[35]Maxwell, JC (1998). *21 Irrefutable Law of leadership,* Nelson Business

[36] Martin Luther King, Jr. "I Have a Dream," delivered 28 August 1963, at the Lincoln Memorial, Washington D.C. http://www.americanrhetoric.com/speeches/mlkihaveadream.htm

[37] Nelson Mandela (1994), *Long walk to Freedom*,. Little, Brown and Company, New York]. p. 624

[38] Carnegie, D (1998). *How to Win Friends and Influence People*, Pocket Books

[39] Gulf War Wikipedia. http://en.wikipedia.org/wiki/Desert_storm